Broken

L.M. Mountford

AF245053

Publisher's Note: This is a work of fiction. Names, characters, places, and incidents are a product of the author's imagination. Locales and public names are sometimes used for atmospheric purposes. Any resemblance to actual people, living or dead, or to businesses, companies, events, institutions, or locales is completely coincidental.

L.M. Mountford -- 1st Ed.
ISBN: 978-1-913945-14-5

About the Author

A self-confessed Tiger fanatic, L.M. Mountford was born and raised in England, first in the town of Bridgewater, Somerset, before later moving to the city of Gloucester where he currently resides. A fully qualified and experienced Scuba Diver, he has travelled across Europe and Africa diving wrecks and seeing the wonders of the world.

He started writing when he was 14. Under the pseudonym Dark Inferno, he has written more than thirty Fanfiction stories.

Other Titles by L.M. Mountford

Collections

The Sweet Temptations Series

Just Friends Series

Broken Heart Series

Stand Alone Titles

DON'T MISS OUT

Sign up for my newsletter and receive weekly updates on my writing progress, cover reveals, public appearances, reviews, and a FREE eBook.

That's right, a free book every week.

And, sometimes even chances to win advanced copies of my next book before anyone else. So, subscribe to my mailing list today, and keep up will all my new releases and special deals, exclusive to my inner circle.

Subscribe via my website

lmmountford.com

BROKEN

LM Mountford

CHAPTER ONE

Damn him! How can he be so good at this? Panting hot lustful breaths as her slender fingers buried themselves in the lush softness of his hair, Vickey tried to fight back her moans as her lover's tongue parted her folds. Swivelling deep, its silky smoothness teased her senses into delirium. Desperate for more, she opened her legs wider, surrendering herself and opening up to him in the most intimate of ways. "Mmm- Ah! Jake! Ahhh! Oh fuck… Please!"

He always knew just where to touch, where to lick, to suck. She couldn't explain it. He just seemed to know how to get her hot, how to have her crying out as the fiery serpent spread from his villainous tongue to coil within her belly, heat seeping through her being in a flood of white-hot pleasure. "Oh! There, right there!"

It was so incredibly delicious, he might just drive her insane.

"That's it love, don't be shy. You love this, don't you? Me eating you. Licking your clit." he whispered, his voice reverberating through her most sensitive spot, feeding her desire. "Want some more?" He blew across her clit, as though to emphasise the question, and the feeling of his warm breath rushing over the pearl, seeming to brush over every nerve in her body, had her bucking and writhing against him, eyes squeezed shut against waves of delirious pleasure.

"Yes. Yes! Don't stop. Don't stop. Don- oh my fucking God! I'm gonna cum!" She gasped, her voice trembling as he buried his

head between her thighs, eating her with a starving hunger, tongue drinking in her flowing nectar before swirling around her clit. Then he was sucking, cheeks hollowing, drawing her little bud from the safety of its hood and into a sensory overload that had her head spinning.

"Open your eyes, angel. Watch me eat your delicious cunt." His words were hot and dirty. She shook her head, the hot knot of tension spiking deliciously at his words and the feeling of his tongue fluttering over her centre. It was too much. Any more and she would shatter. She couldn't take it. She couldn't-

"Open your eyes." He didn't raise his voice. He didn't have to. The command was in his tone and her body obeyed. His eyes gleamed up at her from between her thighs. His hot, predatory gaze burning into hers as that merciless tongue slid over and under. It was so erotic. So...

"Vickey? Hello! You still with us over there?"

Vickey blinked through the haze to find Erika sitting across the table, waving a dainty but expertly manicured hand tipped with silver and white nails. Angela sat beside her, not saying anything, but that sly little grin pulling at the corner of the fiery redhead's mouth spoke volumes. At the very least, it was enough to assure Vickey that her flatmate knew exactly what was going on.

Heat blooming across her face, she dropped her gaze to their table, refusing to meet their eyes. *Dammit, I did it again. What's wrong with me? Why can't I get him out of my head?*

"Geez Vi, you could make a cherry look pale," Erika observed, dropping her hand to take a long sip of her colourful cocktail, draining the glass. "Mmm... that's good. My usual now, Mike," she called to the burly chap behind the bar. Though not exactly their local, they were there just often enough to be called regulars and have a slate for their drinks. They paid off just enough that Mike, the publican, and his staff, would let them slide when they wanted a drink but were having a bad week. Or if they showed off a bit of thigh and asked *nicely*. "So, who brought that blush to your cheeks?"

Vickey shuddered and kept her eyes down, resisting the impulse to touch the heat still burning her skin. The Crown was the quaint, old-fashioned sort of establishment one would expect to find lost in the pages of an Agatha Christie or Jane Austen novel, with a piano in one corner, oak beams running across the ceiling, and a huge old oak bar framed by every sort of bottle and glass. It was a quiet pub where friends could meet and chat after work, but hardly a place to discuss the man haunting her dreams whenever she closed her eyes.

"Oh, I know." Angela cut in. "It's him. Right? The guy you were seeing." The small grin spread into a smile that was surely evil incarnate. "The one you've been pining for."

"Piss off!" Vickey rounded, forcing a smile but she was unable to resist rising to the bait.

The redhead shot a sideways look at Erika and winked. "He's all she thinks about."

"Goddammit Angie!" The heat was practically radiating off her now. "I told you to stop eavesdropping on me when I go to bed!"

"I ain't been droppin' no eaves miss, honest." Angie grinned like the Cheshire Cat, "Wish I could, Vick, but you're a screamer, and I live vicariously." The redhead laughed again as her roommate flipped her the bird.

"Isn't it bad enough you steal my clothes when I'm out? Don't think I don't recognise that top you're flaunting."

Angela's smile dropped. "Aww…come on. You know this looks way cuter on me."

"Is that your idea of an excuse? I know the only reason you want it is so you can show off your tits to every guy who walks by our booth."

"Exactly." She gave an exaggerated wiggle that had her already emphasised breasts jiggling within the confines of the plunging halter that had rhinestones along the hem of the bust. "They get a show, and in return, I get a free drink. Isn't that trade worth your sacrifice?"

"No. I want my top back." Vickey countered dryly, refusing to back down. She needed to stay on the attack and keep the conversation moving.

"What, you want me to strip off right here? In front of everyone?" She grinned and gestured over her shoulder to where a group of lads were clustered around a tallboy. "I know it's Christmas, Vick, but shouldn't I wait to let one of those lucky guys open his present?"

"Don't act like you wouldn't," Vickey countered. "Anyway, I bet it's not something half the guys here haven't opened before."

"You bitch." Angela laughed, only to be checked by the sudden appearance of a fresh tray of drinks.

"Hey girls," A waitress by the name of Autumn greeted. She was a natural head-turner with sun-kissed curls and rosy cheeks, and she was made all the more noticeable by the little two-piece Santa uniform that showed off plenty of thigh and midriff. "These are from the guy over at table thirteen." She shuddered, though made sure to keep it as nonchalant as possible so that only the three other women around the table would notice, before tilting her head. Vickey followed the movement.

At first, it looked like she was indicating to the lads around the tall boy, but the black number nine stamped to the edge of the brass plate suggested otherwise. So instead she looked past the lads to the far end of the pub where a forty-something guy with a greasy top-knot was drooping in a chair. The table's brass plate was marked thirteen.

Following Vickey's gaze, Angela visibly deflated, and it was all Ericka could do not to burst into hysterics. Seeming to sense he had an audience, the guy then turned towards them, smiled and raised his half-a-lager. His broad smile made him look remarkably like Jabba The Hutt and all three girls quickly looked away.

"Thanks," Angela mumbled to Autumn's retreating back, then pushed the drink over to Vickey. "Okay, bad example. But I-"

"Wait a minute!" Erika's eyes were suddenly bright. "You mean that guy, right? The one you said was a marathon man? Looks kinda like a young-ish Sean Bean, only with a goatee. Oh… he was hot, but…" She looked from Angela to Vickey. "Didn't you give him the elbow last month?" *Geez, thanks Erika.*

Immediately aware of both sets of eyes fixing on her, Vickey dropped her gaze down to the drink Angela had passed her. Eyes pricking with tears, she refused to let either woman see her cry and instead focused on the bubbles rising up to pop on the murky top of the Rum and Coke. Had it really only been a month? And to think, they had been so happy.

She had been so happy.

It was such a strange idea, her, happy.

But she had been at the time. That's how it had been with the others. A few dates, that was all, then she'd end things. No attachments. No teary farewells or goodbyes. No commitment. No emotion. It was the best way. Best for her, and most certainly best for them.

And she'd been fine with it every time. They were just men, after all. If necessary, the best parts of them could be replaced by a pair of Triple-A's and a trip to the toy aisle in Ann Summers. But with Jake…

It was madness, pure madness, but in the space of a few weeks, he had completely consumed her in a way no other man had. Made her feel complete and safe. Happy.

Now, he was gone, and it was her fault.

Sipping the rum, she wiped away the tear burning her cheek with the side of her hand.

Angela didn't buy the act for a second. "God, what's with you?"

"What?" Vickey asked, avoiding the redhead's scrutinising stare.

"*What?*" she parroted, then arched a long elegant brow. "Come off it Vick. Don't give us that load of old pony. You never go out with a guy for more than a handful of dates before cutting him out of your life. Then this guy comes along, and you're suddenly attached to him at the hip. You sicken us with a routine that would make Shakespeare tom and dick. Then you break up with him out of the blue. Now I have to drag you out by your hair just to get you to come out for a drink on Christmas Eve." Her smirk dropped. "Seriously, what is it about this guy?"

"It's nothing."

Angela rolled her eyes. "Really? Because I could have sworn that was *The Only Way is Essex* you were watching when I came home."

"I like-"

"You can't stand soaps," Erika countered, cutting her off before she could even finish the lie.

"It's entertaining."

"It's shit."

Vickey shot her another glare but made no effort to defend the program further. A veteran of all things soap, reality, and celebrity TV, if Erika said it was crap, then there was no argument.

She sighed and put her glass down, defeated. "It's nothing. He's… different."

"Different?" Angela asked. "Different how?"

Vickey shrugged. She couldn't explain it. Jake wasn't like other men. Not the kind her friends understood. He was dark and dangerous. Full of that confidence which bordered on arrogance but with that sexy, irresistible bite. Dominating but not overbearing. Scary without terror. He was a complete enigma. Even to her. "Just… different."

Erika and Angela shared a look that made Vickey's belly somersault. She knew that look.

"So, what does he do?" Erika finally asked, taking a long draw on her cider, watching her across the glass.

Vickey blinked. "I… I don't know"

"He didn't tell you?" Angela leant forward, scrutinising.

"I never asked."

"But how come?"

And there it was, the question that she dreaded. How could she tell them she was afraid to ask? Afraid of what his answer might be?

Vickey wasn't a liar. She'd grown up with liars. She'd learnt to lie before she could walk. She was possibly one of the greatest liars who'd ever lived. She'd seen the hurt they caused. She hated lying. She certainly didn't want to lie to two of the only true friends she'd ever had, but she'd seen the truth.

Jake never made a big deal about her finding it that time, but it was there.

Stashed away in his drawer, between a packet of paracetamol and a box of condoms.

A SIG Sauer P226.

Only certain men carried those. And none of them worked jobs that made good gossip. Good, healthy gossip anyway.

"It just never came up," Vickey shrugged, trying to appear nonchalant. "But he works a lot of strange hours and keeps himself in shape. Not very toned, but healthy, like he does a lot of running. And his stamina is amazing, so maybe he's a personal trainer." That at least was a half-truth. She'd never liked those muscle-bound guys. They were so heavy and slow, all show and no bite. Jake had been just her type, tall and lean but with muscle in all the right places.

Erika shot Angela a knowing sideways look. "Maybe he's married."

The words were like a cold shiver down Vickey's spine. "What?"

Angela didn't miss a beat. "Yeah, he's married and seeing you on the side."

"No."

"Well, where does he live?" asked Ericka, now beaming.

"I don't... I think in one of those new towers they built on the East End a couple of years ago. But he only took me there a couple of times and I never paid much attention."

Where did he live? The cabby had always been waiting for them and she'd always been too *preoccupied* to pay much attention to where he was taking her.

"He's married."

Vickey grit her teeth, growing angry with that smug smile playing across her roommate's peach coloured lips. "No, he's not."

Angela gave her a withering look. "Oh, have a day off Vick. He doesn't tell you anything about himself, works weird hours, takes you back to a flat that could be anywhere in the city for all you know- "

"What about his phone?" Erika asked.

Vickey rounded on her. "What about it?"

"W-was he on it a lot?" Her friend seemed to shrink under her glare. "Did he ever try and hide it from you, refuse to let you use it or-"

"No, Erika. I never asked to use his phone and he never made a big deal out of it. He's not married, so just drop it." Knowing she needed to calm dawn, Vickey grabbed the Rum and Coke and took a drink. It didn't help. "And what does it matter now? It's over, remember? I broke it off. Not him. Me!"

"It's nothing to be ashamed of," Erika pressed on regardless, though changing tact, as if worried that the accusations had somehow insulted her. "You certainly wouldn't be the first. My mum once met this guy who had a girlfriend and a wife, he… he told them all he drove juggernauts so they wouldn't-"

"He's not married!" Vickey snapped, with more certainty than she had any right to have. The hot ice of her tone cutting off any remaining argument Erika might have had and made her friend's eyes drop down to stare at the now empty cider glass.

Vickey immediately regretted being so sharp with her. She hadn't meant to be, but she couldn't help it. He wasn't married, she just knew it. Men lying about their marriage didn't turn up with the sorts of bruises Jake would sprout overnight. Or look at her the way he had; as if he were looking into her, to the centre of her being. No one had ever looked at her that way before. *He can't be married. He just can't!*

Angela nervously cleared her throat. "What did he think about your dad's breakout?"

"He didn't know."

"But… how?" Erika looked up, surprise written across her face. "Your dad's escape from Belmarsh was all over the news."

"I told him my surname's Romano. It was my mother's maiden name."

"So, you never…" Ericka paused.

"What?"

Angela leaned forward, voice hushed. "Told him about your family?"

Vickey snorted "Of course not. God, what do you suggest? Shag him senseless, then go, *Hey, babe, that was wild.*

Oh, by the way, you know that escaped murderer who's been all over the news? That's my dad. I've heard some crazy pillow talk, but that about takes the biscuit. Then just for kicks, I could add, *'And if the wrong person sees us together, Terrance Daley is likely to cut your cock off and feed you your balls'.*" She gave another dry laugh, then threw back the remains of the Rum and Coke, ignoring the way her friends exchanged worried looks at the mention of Daley.

Forty years ago, Terrance Daley - or just Terry to his friends, the River Police, Flying Squad, and Daily Mail readers- had been an infamous enforcer of Freddie Foreman. Five years ago, The Mail had called him The People's King of London, but Vickey had only ever known him as *Uncle Terry*.

Suddenly she was there again. In that room. The night cold and crawling over her skin, fingers grasping her chin, sour breath reeking of whisky hissing in her ear. *"Good girl, now lie down on the bed and let Uncle Terry see…"*

"Jesus! Vickey…Vickey!" Angela and Erika stood around her. "You're as white as sheet."

"What's wrong? You feelin' alright?"

"Y… yeah. I'm fine." *Christ, where did that come from?*

She shook her head, trying to clear the fog, and suddenly was all too aware of the sweat clinging to her brow. Then, she realised just about every head in the bar was watching their table. "Listen… I've got to go."

"What?"

"Where are you going-"

"Are you sure you're-"

"Want us to come-"

"Maybe we should get you checked out-"

She shook them off. "No. No, I'm fine." Grabbing her jacket from the back of the chair, she slung her handbag over a shoulder. "I just need some air. To think. Yeah. I'll see you later." Then, eyes glassy and heart pounding, she was moving past a shaken Autumn, round the bar, and through the door into the winter night.

CHAPTER TWO

Christmas was only a couple of hours away and to mark the holiday, *Seven* had been decked in blue and white. Projectors in the ceiling made it look as if snowflakes were falling around the dancers who were writhing together through the clouds of dry ice fog enveloping the floor.

The floor-to-ceiling windows of the manager's office made up the wall overlooking the dance floor. However, the view was lost on Jake. *Are you down there?*

The throngs were pressed so tight together, it was virtually impossible to tell one person from the next, but he could imagine her down there, writhing and gyrating to the beat against a faceless male, hot and eager…

His fingers twitched at the thought and he had to force down the impulse to reach for the sidearm hidden beneath his leather ¾ jacket. Though the P226 was his weapon of choice, the lighter, smaller, standard-issue Glock 17 was the more practical choice when it came to these messenger-boy jobs. Not only was it lighter and more easily concealed under a jacket, its all-polymer design meant it was less likely to set off the basic security systems and metal detectors found in civilian recreational areas.

Get a grip, man. It was ridiculous. He was being ridiculous. A slip of a girl, barely in her twenties. What had he expected? Marriage and happily ever after? Those were nothing but fantasies when you joined the Squad. Hell, if she hadn't broken it off, he soon would have. For her sake if not his. She deserved better.

"Well, well, well…"

Shit! Jake had his hand in his jacket, thumb flipping the catch of the shoulder holster strap and his palm fastening round the textured grip of the Glock in the moment it took his head to whip back.

He relaxed, slightly, when he saw who was standing in the office's door.

"When Mr Margrave said he was sending someone, I certainly wasn't expecting it to be you of all people, Jake Talbert."

"I wasn't his first choice." Jake agreed, letting his hand fall to his side. At five feet six and shaped like a propped-up bag of suet in a black, hand-made, three-piece suit, with a receding mop of hair more grey than black that curled at the sides and a pudgy face, Henry Yate was not what anyone would consider threatening. "But your message said it was urgent, and it's Christmas Eve. The rest of the Flying Squad have plans, so here I am."

Yate moved around the desk to sit back in the padded swivel chair with legs crossed and hands steepled in his lap. The pose was supposed to appear relaxed but only made his hands look like a bustle of fat little sausages. "I heard you weren't about much these days. Word is, it's been a busy couple of weeks for you."

"They've had their moments."

"I'll say. Intimidating witnesses. Assaulting suspects. Not to mention beating that poor bugger half to death in a billiards hall. And in front of witnesses." Pearly whites glinted as he fixed Jake with a smile that would very likely curdle milk. "I heard you're out of control. Something about a bird blowing you out, giving you the Dear John routine. So now you're under investigation, chained to a desk. You know, in these times of civil unrest, it's a real comfort to know those brave boys in blue take the time to remember their duty and professional integrity. If only all law enforcement took such time to protect us law-abiding citizens from the filth that walks our streets."

"And here I thought you drove everywhere nowadays?"

Yate's smile dropped. "Touché."

"Well, I wouldn't let my unpredictability and violent tendencies bother you," Jake said, with forced nonchalance as he walked around the desk to sit in the chair opposite the older man. These games were all part of the routine. "I had a bad break. I needed to vent, and that wanker in the hall decided to be a smart arse. So, we played a game of doctor." He shrugged, leaning back and folding his arms. "He lost."

"Yes, those clips on YouTube made that obvious. Shame they didn't also show the firearm he allegedly had concealed on his person."

"You know, the enquiry's psychologist remarked on that too, but it's hard to argue with evidence found on the scene."

"Unless it's a plant."

There was an adequate response to that, but Jake had to force himself not to bite. Yate was little more than a two-bit snitch, a common rogue with a number of dodgy businesses who made it his business to have all twenty little sausage digits in every dirty, bent, and stolen pie in London, and an ear to the ground in all the right and wrong places. He was the owner and manager of *Seven*, but it was a smokescreen, a bit of cloak and dagger, something to look good on the self-assessment. Yate's true business was information, and he didn't discriminate. It was no secret he sold to both the villains and the law of London but, because he never went too far and always threw both sides a bone, he was untouchable.

And the powers-that-be had decreed Jake must play this stupid fat fucker's little games.

Yate went on. "Of course, your recent recommendation for the Saint George might have had something to do with that."

Jake's eyes narrowing. *Now, just how did you learn about that, you slimy bastard?*

"D-notices aren't what they use to be." Yate grinned, apparently reading his thoughts. "Out of curiosity, you killed how many Jihadists? Ten?"

"Six," Jake snarled.

"Six," Yate parroted, his smile broad and knowing. "Quite a bit of luck you had there. And at such an opportune time. Extraordinary. I bet that put those CID boys out of joint. All that effort they went through to conceal the Browning. They finally have your balls in a vice, then you go and pull a stunt like that and the Chief Constable himself tells them to put it-"

"Yate!" Though he did not raise his voice above a whisper, Jake's tone was sharper than a razor. "I have better things to do than listen to you crow all night. Now, are you going to tell me what's so important that I had to come over here on Christmas Eve, or do I have to drag you down to lockup for the night for wasting my time?"

Yate smiled, knowing he'd won this round. "Terry's planning a score."

"*The People's King*? You do surprise me," Jake said in a tone dripping with sarcasm. "You'll have to do better than that. He's legit, remember?"

"Yes, but all jobs still require his seal of approval. This is still his town," Yate pointed out. "There isn't a major heist goin' down in the borough that hasn't received his nod of approval."

"That may be, but that amounts to conspiracy, at best, and it's bloody hard to get a conspiracy conviction without rock-solid evidence." Jake eased back into the chair. "Everyone knows Terry's in it up to his neck. Half the MET is working to drag him down off his podium and the other half are in his pocket. I know that whenever I arrive on the scene, Terry has his fingers in it, then flaunts his immunity by building a new wing to the children's hospital on the proceeds. But so long as every villain I drag in keeps swearing he's the mastermind, I can't touch him. And no one is going to stand up in the Old Bailey, point to Terry Daley, and go 'that's him, your honour. That's the geeza'. Nobody's that stupid. Not after what happened to Stanton's kid."

"After his fall he was drawn to the block, and there his bowels withdrawn, and he was divided into four parts," Yate recited. "Such a terrible way to die. And so young. They say Terrance himself gave Mad Dog the order." Suddenly Yate's small, watery rat-like eyes were fixed on Jake. The, his smile suddenly mocking, he went on. "To prove his loyalty, he butchered his own son before the boy could give evidence against Daley. Then murdered his wife for protecting him. Now he's on the run. Tell me, did they ever find his daughter?"

A cold hand settled around Jake's heart at the mention of the Stanton girl.

He'd heard the stories of Terrance Daley's playroom. It was an underworld myth. A fabrication. Probably cooked up by Daley himself to add terror to his infamy. Even so, there were some things it didn't bear thinking about.

"Such a sweet girl." Yate pressed. "The boy I can almost understand, but to think a father might knowingly hand his own innocent child over to tha-"

"*Harry*, I'm beginning to lose my rag with you." Emphasising Yate's Christian name with deadly purpose, Jake had to force himself to stay calm. "The Flying Squad was formed to tackle commercial armed and unarmed robberies. Not chase leads on escaped convicts playing truant. Mad Dog Jack Stanton is a murderer, a thug, and an extortionist. He demands money with menaces and makes bodies disappear. He doesn't get tilled to the nines and wave water pistols at cashiers' heads." He pushed up from the chair, braced his hands on the desk's leather top and leant forward to look the other man square in the eye. "If you have information on where he might be hiding, I suggest you dial 999. Otherwise, unless you give me something tangible, you'll be drinking your Christmas dinner through a straw in intensive care."

There were tricks to a good threat. It was all about the perceived capability of violence. A man with his gun out but shaking like a fairy was just as likely to piss his pants as carry it through and the world could see it. But the smallest gesture, the right look, transformed a man into a monster. And from him, a good threat was deadlier than any muscle-bound gorilla with a shooter.

Deflating like a punctured balloon under the younger man's cold blue glare, Yate pulled open a desk drawer and pulled out a pocket voice recorder that he placed on the leather top. Easing back into his seat, Jake eyed the device suspiciously, before nodding. "Go on…"

Moving so quickly he almost fell out of his seat, Yate pawed the device like a monkey trying to open a fiddly banana, his fingers thumbing the recorder until he finally managed to find the Play button. Someone had obviously prepared it in advance because no sooner had he depressed the trigger then Terrance Daley's old, scratchy voice, heavily flavoured by the East End, began to speak, caught in the midst of giving some oration that would have given dear old Adolf a turn.

"Shut it off," Jake said after about twenty minutes. "Is this genuine?"

"Oh yes," Yate confirmed, taking a long draw on his cigar before placing it on the ashtray and stopping the recording. He had fully regained his composure. "Terrance booked my back room for a little Christmas function for a few colleagues. So, I arranged for a few of these to be placed here and there shortly after he arrived. Very good at that sort of thing, are my girls."

"Well, that's very interesting *Harry*. I'm very impressed. In fact, I'm just fucking astounded. You got Terry on tape. Talking with a lot of people who may or may not be villains, discussing a heist any criminal in Greater London will probably be discussing tonight, or his plans to move a bookcase, repaint his bathroom, kitchen, or Saint Paul's bloody fucking cathedral. I mean…" Jake's eyes narrowed. "What the hell is wrong with you? You fucking idiot. How could you be so fuckin' stupid?"

Yate's mouth gaped. "I-I don't understand."

"Oh, you don't? Well, let me enlighten you, you tart. It's shit, Yate. This. Is. Shit!" Jake pronounced the last three words with a deadly emphasis. "There are no names. No times, dates, not even a damn street address. He's meticulous about avoiding saying anything that can link him to any crime, past or currently in the works. I can't get a warrant based on this. I couldn't even get planning permission. Will you wear a wire?"

"Me?" The older man visibly paled, horrified by the suggestion. "Good Lord, no. I'm not… I mean, I couldn't. Daley would kill me. He'd throw me to his dogs."

"You're a lying, cheating pimp, Yate," Jake growled. "Not only have you not given me probable cause, but by recording this and playing it for me, you've made it so that any case I try and start based on it will be thrown out for illegal tapping, invasion of privacy, and God knows what else his high-priced brief can dream up. He might even try and drag you up on charges. You want to take that chance? Because I assure you Terrance will."

Yate was suddenly so white he looked like he was about to be sick and his lip was practically trembling. "No."

"That's what I thought." Rising up out of his chair, Jake walked around the desk to stand in front of Yate and snatched the recorder from his chubby fingers. "You drag me over here again for this bullshit and I'll hand this tape over to The People's King myself." He turned on his heel to leave.

"What? No… you can't!"

"Watch me."

The switch was concealed in the same drawer that Yate had stored the recorder. A panic button that when triggered, activated the alarm in the office's concealed side room. It only took a moment for Yate to trigger the switch and another for the door disguised as a bookcase to swing open.

They were dressed like twins in matching black suits and came sulking out like well-trained dogs. One going right. The other left. Circling.

The first minder was a monster of a man. An immense six-foot-five brute, more than twenty stone of muscle, with blond hair cropped short and a bushy tash under a nose that was squashed and crooked from numerous breaks.

The second was nearly as tall, but where his companion was all raw power, this one was lean and wiry, broad-chested but long-limbed and narrow-hipped, like a chimpanzee that had learned to walk upright. He had the face of a monkey to match with long dark hair, large round eyes, and a big toothy grin that Jake had the immediate urge to slap off his face.

"Well, look who it is, Pinky and Perky. What's the matter boys, CBeebies give you the axe?" Jake asked, stopping in the very centre of the room as both men came to a pause, one at his front and the other his back. His mind raced, trying to put a name to a face, but he didn't recognise either of them.

Not from this manor. Now, why would the stupid fat bastard be getting outside muscle?

"Is this fella giving you hassle Mr Yate?" the monster asked in a deep, near unintelligible drawl that could only have come from the Welsh Valleys.

The other's grin stretched almost ear to ear, making him look all the more like a primate. "Would you like us to escort him out for you sir?" *No doubt there, a fucking Scouser! No wonder he looks like a monkey.*

Yate was out of his chair and pointing frantically at Jake. "That… that recorder, it's mine. I want it. Stop him!"

Yate, you really are a stupid fat bastard. Jake shot the older man a cold, narrow-eyed look as he twisted, trying to keep both minders in view.

The Welshman stepped forward, hand outstretched. "I'm gonna have to take that from you."

"This is police business," Jake growled, twisting to face the bigger man. "You boys scuttle back to your cage before someone gets a slap."

The Liverpudlian moved closer, cracking his knuckles. "Ha, would you get a load of this tosser. Old Bill? He's as much Old Bill as me ma's the Duchess of Cambridge. Oh, and didn' that sound like hostility to you, Jones?"

"That it did. And we don't like hostility, do we, Tim?" They both grinned; as if the very thought of a fight made them giddy. "Now, I don't think you heard me. I'm afraid I must insist, mate. Or I'm going to take it."

Jake's gaze darted from Jones, to Tim, and then back to the Welshman. *Tim and Jones? More like Bill and bleedin' Ben.*

"Well, looks like you're not giving me much choice…" He held the recorder up for them to see, then out as if about to pass it to Jones, only to pocket it. "Well, come and get it."

They came at him as one.

Though Tim was the faster, it was Jones who reached Jake first, a titanic fist curling through the air. The punch should have hit him dead in the side of his head, just behind his ear, a blow almost certain to stun, if not knock out. Except, the smaller man side-stepped, so it passed by harmlessly, before sticking his foot out, tripping the big man, then slipping down and under Tim's attack. That should have left the smaller of the two men open, but he had not devoted himself fully to the attack and his reflexes were good enough to check himself as he went, countering Jake's riposte by twisting away, keeping his delicate flank out of the line of attack.

Jake didn't wait. This was the more dangerous of the two, the faster and more controlled. He had to be put down hard and fast. Or he'd let the Welshman take the lead, using the bigger man as a shield whilst he attacked from all around. So, Jake came on hard, his first punch a winding jab to the throat, sending the Liverpudlian reeling. Jake followed with his second attack, a devastating phoenix fist to the solar-plexus that had the slightly bigger man doubling over, opening him up for a *coup de grâce*.

And then it was over.

The punch slid past the ribs and into the liver with such a force that it had Tim crumpling to the floor like a sack of potatoes as Jake, his only means of support, slid away. The monkey grin was gone, replaced by a twisted grimace of agony as colour bled into his face and he writhed on the floor, desperately trying to draw in the breath to scream.

It took all of three moves to put the Liverpudlian down. Three moves. Three blows. Three moments.

Jones was just clambering back to his feet when Jake turned to him. Red-faced, the big Welshman's eyes moved back and forth between Jake and the writhing heap on the floor. He wanted to attack but had been unnerved by his associate's quick dispatch. Now his mind was working, weighing the odds.

Jake couldn't help his grin. At barely seven metres squared, Yate's office would never have been his first choice to fight such an uncommonly large man. Space and speed were vital when fighting stronger men. Should he trip over a piece of furniture or become entangled with the brute, he was as good as dead. But an unsure or angry foe was far more likely to make mistakes.

"Alright. Come on! Come on sheep shagger! Bah! Bah!" Jake mocked.

That did the trick.

Bellowing with what could have been an instinctive hatred that all Celts retain for their Saxon neighbours and oppressors, Jones lunged. And Jake let him. Let him come in close. Let him close the gap, then parried the coming blow with a sweep of his arm that deflected Jones's punch as Jake stepped in with one of his own straight between the bigger man's eyes. Bone knuckled bone as the Welshman's charge drove him onto the blow, crushing the already crumpled cartilage in his nose so that it seemed to explode in crimson, before Jake's follow-up kick sent him stumbling into the back of a leather sofa.

With a colossal hand pressed to the bloodied mess of his face, Jones glared back at Jake before his eyes darted sideways to an end table, upon which stood, well within arm's reach, a foot-tall sculpture of the Venus de Milo. He sidestepped, hand outstretched.

"Don't you bloody dare." The Glock was in Jake's hand, sights trained on the pulped ruin that had been the Welshman's nose.

Jones froze. "Don… Don't shoot."

"Then don't make me. Keep them up, yes, that's it, above the shoulders." Jake advanced forward slowly. "Now, Sunshine, I'm afraid this is either about to get very messy or go very, very…"

The Paras could teach a man just about everything there was to know about blood and pain, but nothing ever really beat the classics. So, he settled for kneeing the bigger man in the balls. "Bad for you."

Eyes rolling, Jones's knees buckled, and he slumped to the ground unconscious

"Not so big now, are you?" Grinning, Jake holstered the pistol and, without sparing a glance back at the Welshman, turned on his heel and stepped over the equally unconscious Tim.

Yate could barely contain himself. "Sergeant! Wait! No… Jimmy Dawson"

Jake paused, hand outstretched to grasp the door handle. He threw a backwards look across his shoulder. "What about him?"

"He was there. He'll talk to you."

"Dawson's no grass." Jake's eyes narrowed.

"No. But he's angry at Terry. Reckons Daley owes him because he kept his mouth shut and did his bird when some geezer from the regional crime squad offered him an early release from Brixton. In exchange for pointing the finger at Terry."

"That's all they offered?"

"Well, that and the arresting officer's head on a plate."

Jake barked with laughter. "Ha! I bet they bloody did. I knew it, the sneaky slags. So why would Jimmy talk to me and not them?"

"Why?" Yate looked as if the younger man had grown a second head. "Because if he talks to the regional boys, Terry will know it before the end of the hour. Angry or not, Daley scares the shit out of poor little Jimmy."

"Just about every villain in London is terrified of Terry, and most of the coppers on the manor as well, it's how the bastard stays on top. Get to the point."

"Why you? Well, you're the guy who put him in Brixton in the first place. He spent most of his sentence there in a wheelchair on your account. If you go to him, make him see reason, he'll probably do whatever you want."

"And if he declines?"

Harry shrugged "Wheelchairs are still covered under the NHS."

Jake laughed again, then reached back into his jacket, pulled out the recorder and threw it to Yate. The fat man just managed to catch the device. "Merry Christmas, Yate. I'll be in touch."

Chapter Three

On any other night, the Docklands would have been a bustling hive of people and cars. But with less than an hour until Christmas, most of the inhabitants of London were already indoors.

Immune to the chilly December night, Vickey let her feet carry her, not really caring where. She just needed to… to what?

She'd told Erica and Angela she wanted to think. But that wasn't true, she couldn't bear to think. Thinking led to memories. And those memories always led her back to *him*.

It had been so long since the last time. She'd almost forgotten how painful the memories could be. *Ten years on, but one wrong thought and I'm right back there again.*

Why did it have to happen now, when she was already so messed up from Jake?

No, she couldn't go there. Couldn't bear to even think about *him*.

So, she walked and walked, until she finally came to one of the many redeveloped warehouses that infested the ancient city. But where others had been reborn as luxury flats, shopping complexes, and heritage sites, this single red brick structure remained much as it had done a hundred years ago but for a bright neon sign above the door that said in bold red letters *Seven*.

Vickey had heard the name before. Erika had mentioned it once or twice. A club?

Suddenly she knew what she needed to do.

Chapter Four

Jake wasn't a drinker by nature and never touched a drop when he was on the job. He'd seen too many good mates go down bad roads that way. Drink might be a soldier's best friend away from the lines, however it could seriously fuck up a career quicker than a Rupert with a chip on his shoulder if not kept in check.

But he was off the clock, and he seriously needed a drink.

The server behind the bar, an obvious toff with blond hair gelled into what Jake could only describe as a failed bird's nest, only looked at him when he ordered a Black and Tan. It took three tries before he finally got the cocktail right.

"That'll be eleven forty-five, *sir*," he said with an obviously forced smile as he placed the infusion on the bar.

Jake all but gaped as he fished in his jean's pocket for his wallet. "Eleven forty-fucking-five? I asked for a drink, not the time. Where did you get the beer, Japan?" Indignant, he put a twenty-pound note on the bar and scooped up the glass. "You could have at least made it a pint."

The toff ignored the jab and took the note over to the till before bringing him his change. "Can I get you anything else?"

"At twelve quid a beer, not bloody likely." But the server had already gone to another patron, so Jake just shoved the change back into his pocket and twisted round to face the dance floor. Leaning back, he sipped the B&T, watching, instinctively looking for something he was utterly terrified of finding.

They'd met in a place just like this. She'd been working as a waitress in the club and he'd been out for a celebratory drink with the rest of the squad. She'd taken their drinks and he'd engaged with a bit of banter. It had been completely innocent, but then they'd crossed paths in his regular cafe where he went for his tea break when staying in HQ. Then again at the end of the week when he'd been grabbing a ready-meal and she'd been on the till. It turned out she worked in a temp agency. It had been the end of her shift and seeing his choice of cuisine, she'd offered to make him dinner if he would walk her home. It might have been more banter, but it hadn't stopped him from offering to drive her.

The age gap wasn't an issue. He'd never asked why she never accepted the frequent offers of permanent employment from her numerous temp jobs. She'd never asked about his job or why he kept 'illegal' firearms in his drawer or had to leave suddenly sometimes, or why he always came back with cuts and bruises that would make Mike Tyson think twice. They'd just clicked.

Goddamnit, get a grip man. She's gone. She left. You're done. Get over it-

He froze.

There she was. Vickey Romano, gyrating on the dance floor in tight skinny jeans that drew every eye to her luscious derriere and a long-sleeved, halter-style sweater that stretched across her cleavage while showing off her milky midriff.

Fuck, she was gorgeous. So gorgeous, just seeing her tore at him, made his heart skip and his cock hard.

Her dancing was a thing to behold. Graceful. Seductive. Neither slow nor fast, but a pace that was entirely her own and utterly bewitching. She gave it her all, moving her hands up her body, through her long raven locks, to join over her head as she rocked her hips and abdomen, inviting someone, anyone, to come hither.

He watched her from his perch at the bar. Drinking in her every move and contour, observing her the way a falcon watches a rabbit in the meadow, but in the back of his mind, he remembered the feeling of those long legs wrapped around him. Those delicate fingers on his skin, in his hair, urging him on as he devoured her luscious pussy. Remembered the softness of her raven locks sliding through his fingers, the heat of her skin on his, the taste of her rosy nipples, the kittenish moans she made whenever he fingered her clit while fucking her from behind…

He wanted her regardless. Wanted to go over and kiss her, take her, mark her somehow so all the world knew she was his.

He tossed back and drained the Tan & Black. *Utrinque Paratus.*

If it weren't for the seasonal décor, one could almost have been forgiven for thinking it was anything other than a national holiday in less than an hour. *Seven* was bustling. The music was loud. The atmosphere sultry. And the patrons were hot and heavy.

Utterly consumed by the beat and flow of the music, Vickey let it sweep her away. She wanted to lose herself in the music, forget the pain, the loneliness.

This was what she'd needed. This freedom. The momentary release of knowing she was lost, just one amongst many. A girl like any other. *They* couldn't touch her here. There were no hunters in the crowd. No one looking to claim the bounty on her head. No hunters, just watchers.

She could feel eyes on her from somewhere, hot and hungry, raking her from head to toe.

And suddenly the music blaring out through the speakers changed. The chronic pop Christmas song switched to the sensual throb of a jazz storm, making her very core vibrate to its seductive rhythm.

It's true what they say,
Love is blind,
so, we must find our way.

You know my name
Come into my world,
See through my eyes.
Hear my words,
And know what I say

Remember
We've been dreaming this life
But when you need me
I'll hold you close
Hold you tight

Love you forever
As we're together this night
I'm broken without you...

The eyes never left her as she let the music guide her, giving herself over to its sensual beat as the heat raked her from head to toe, sizzling across her skin. It was as thrilling as it was unnerving.

Exaggerating the swing of her hips, Vickey did a slow three-sixty, her eyes glancing left and right. Where was he? Her watcher? She could feel him, close by, and getting closer. Weaving between all these bodies, using the tight press to conceal himself. A predator, but not the kind she was used to. She could see that sort easily enough, leering at her over their date's shoulder or over a glass, like dogs after a bone. Obvious. Pathetic. But this guy?

He was different. Exciting. It felt like she was dancing for him. Just for him.

Maybe she'd even let him pick her up, take her home. It had been weeks since she'd last gotten laid, and she needed it. Needed to bury these feelings. A hot, hard fuck had always been good for that, good for burying the pain and letting her forget, if only for a moment. Jake had been so good at that.

No, forget him. He's a guy, just another guy. A big, hard dick with powerful hands and a wicked tongue. She didn't need him. *Any of the rogues here would do-*

A shiver of awareness rippled up her spine, then hands were on her- large, powerful hands, enveloping her, rough fingers tingling across the skin of her belly, drawing her against a male body.

It's true what they say,
Love is blind,
so, we must find our way.

As we play this game
A game of lies

You know my name
You know my world
I am yours
So, you are mine

Remember
We've been dreaming this life
But when you need me
I'll hold you close
Hold you tight

Love you forever
As we're together this night
I'm broken without you
So, let's forget the lies
Break the wheel
And return to the light.

Something inside Vickey yielded under the aroma of raw masculinity, fogging her thoughts. The guy smelled of leather, sweat, and… something else, something so familiar it made her core throb. His hands were everywhere and nowhere. Brushing over her midriff, along the hem of her jeans, and up her ribs, exploring practically every bit of skin he could reach, ferreting out the spots that had her tingling at his touch. Still caught in the song's beat, she arched like a cat into his touch, arms reaching back to encircle his neck, grinding against his groin, the weight of his arousal pressing along the curve of her derriere.

"Mmm… naughty girl," he growled in her ear, close enough that she could hear him over the music but far enough away that she could feel his words on the slope of her neck. The words sent delicious shivers down her spine. *That voice! That voice!* She tried to turn, to face him, but he held her firmly, pressed tight against his body with the subtle dominance that drove her wild. *No, it couldn't be, not here, not him!*

Then her mind went blank.

He was kissing her. Small, hot little kisses up her neck to the spot just beneath her ear, making her knees weak and pussy throb, yearning for attention. She matched him, pushing back, rubbing against him, relishing the feel of his hard body, her hands reaching, exploring the muscular ridge of his back and shoulders, nails biting whenever her teased *that* spot.

He was working her into a state, and utterly absorbed in the feelings his mouth was conjuring, she almost didn't notice him fingering the fastenings of her jeans, popping the button.

"No!" she half gasped, half moaned, panic rising in her breast. This was going too far, he wouldn't.

"Relax. Just go with it." He pushed, suckling her pulse spot.

"Oh God."

He was insane. There were too many people. Anyone could see. All it would take was one glance, a curious look, but the risk only made her hotter. And the thought of it, getting finger-fucked here, in the middle of this club in Wapping, on the dance floor, surrounded by all these people practically dripping with lust, had her legs spreading, giving his wandering fingers licence to slip into her jeans, beneath her panties.

Remember
I'm there for you
our love will always be true

It's true what they say,

"You're so wet."

She could practically hear his smirk as he ever so gently brushed a finger across her folds. Not hard enough to enter her, but still enough to collect some of the creamy dew seeping down her thighs and tease across her clit in small circles.

Her moan was throaty and desperate, her hips rolled, seeking more contact. "Someone might see."

"Yes, and that makes you hot, doesn't it?" he growled in her ear, so close and low now it was entirely dangerous and exciting, like sex given voice. "The thought of being watched, of getting caught…"

Goosebumps rose all over her body. The music was loud, reverberating around the club, blending into white noise amidst the holler of the bodies enveloping them, but Vickey's attention was fixed on that voice. She didn't miss a word, his every syllable pushing her into sensory overload as those fingers, those damn wicked fingers, rubbed up and down her slit. He applied just that little bit of extra pressure each time he touched her clit and then dragged his finger downward, until she could feel her body opening, his fingertip dragging along her inner tissues.

"Don't!" she whispered in a voice much too husky to pretend she didn't want this, want him.

Whilst one hand was doing such wicked unspeakable things with her pussy, the other was reaching up, coarse fingers sliding up under the hem of her sweater to brush the underside of her breasts, teasing and feather-soft. It turned her nipples to stiff, almost painful peaks yearning for attention. She didn't need to look to know her arousal was visible through her sweater.

"No! We can't mmm…Stop… Don't stop. No!" Her body throbbed and clenched around his finger when it pushed inside, penetrating her to the knuckle, and she made no effort to hide her wanton grinding on his palm.

Vickey should have been embarrassed, even ashamed of her responsiveness. She was letting this complete stranger do and say these naughty things to her, but he was right. Just the thought of doing these things here, in such a public place, where anyone could see… It was more than just thrilling, it was pure addiction, a fire in her blood that drove her wild.

"That's it, love. Feels good, doesn't it?"

Panting from the feelings he was evoking inside her, she stubbornly shook her head, refusing to answer.

"Oh?" Though he tried to sound abashed, his hold on her never slacked and she could practically hear the grin in his voice. The sexy bastard was enjoying this, enjoying baiting her and making her bend to his whim. "If you want me to stop…" He began to withdraw.

"No!" Her thighs snapped shut around his hand.

"Oh? So, you want *more*?" His finger curled inside her, swirling leisurely, stroking her insides.

"Yes!" It felt like an eternity since anyone had done this to her. Jake had been the last, and she would have given anything in the world for it to be him in this anonymous creature's place, his hands stroking her, fingers inside her. But Jake was gone, off somewhere else, probably fucking some lucky little tart. She'd seen to that. So now she had to make her bed, and shag in it until dawn until she'd worn herself out on this walking dildo.

And he was quite a dildo indeed. Hard as steel and straining quite vividly against the fabric of his jeans, she could practically feel the heat of him radiating through their clothes. The weight of his desire pushed up against her, grinding in that all so delicious way that had her rocking and grinding, fucking herself on his hand. "Yes! More! I want…more!"

"Naughty girl," he purred, the low throb of his voice coursing through her as she thrust against his single digit, trying to incite him. Then her mind was blank, lost in a whiteout as his mouth fell upon hers, swallowing her moan as he pushed a second digit inside her, thumb pad rubbing circles over and around her clit. And all the while his tongue mimicked the movement of his fingers, swirling and spinning, flitting in and out of her hot cavern.

It was too much.

Too good.

Then suddenly he was gone.

No! Maddened from her closeness, her eyes snapped open to meet a hauntingly familiar pair of cool blue eyes. "Jake."

He'd let his hair grow out until it almost reached his shoulders and shaved his goatee. But there was no doubt. It was him.

"Hello, angel." He grinned that devastating grin that never failed to make her wet for him and had her thighs rubbing together of their own volition, desperate to rekindle the contact he was denying her. "Does it really turn you on so much? Getting finger-fucked here? Where anyone could see? Maybe some already have…" The dishevelled look suited him. Made him look younger, enhancing the strong lines of his jaw, and, if it was possible, even more dangerous when combined with his black leather jacket, jeans and shirt. "How 'bout we really give them a show?" And to her horror, he brought his hand to his lips, the hand that had just been buried in her jeans, buried inside her, and licked one slick and shiny finger- tasting her in the middle of the crowded dance floor.

She came.

Remember
I'm broken without you
You want to save me
But together we're stronger
Together
What's broken can be fixed
But my love for you
Will never die.

Chapter Five

This was a very bad idea.

He'd only gone up to talk to her, but then…

The shadowy back corner didn't offer much cover, but it was quieter here and they were far enough out of the way, hidden behind a private booth, that Jake was confident nobody could see. He had pinned her to the wall, hands braced, penning her in with his body as their tongues danced a fiery duet and her fingers clutched at his jacket.

"This…this is… we should stop…" she gasped, tearing her lips from his. Her objections, however only opened more skin for him to kiss so he dipped down to ravish the slope of her neck with nips and licks while working his way between her legs. Needing her to feel how hard she'd gotten him. And he was hard. Hemmed in by the tight confines of his denim prison, his cock felt like a solid length of steel between his legs. The pressure amassing inside wasn't exactly painful, but by no means was it pleasant either.

It demanded release, and he fully intended to grant that wish. Later.

"Mmm… but you're so wet," he whispered, gently nipping the spot where her neck and collar met before soothing it with a slow, leisurely lick. "Come on, say you want me. Your needy little pussy must be throbbing for my cock."

Arching into his mouth, Vickey fisted his hair, pulling him closer. "No, no! Jake! Please…"

She was nervous, her voice low and breathless, still worried they'd be caught, but that wanton tone was music to his ears. He collared both her wrists in one hand, pinning them behind her back with enough force to make her gasp.

"Ah. Ah. Ah… No touching." He was sinking to his knees, the fingers of his free hand curling into the waistband of her jeans.

"Jake?" she gasped, louder now, as the denim pooled around her boots, exposing her to his hungry eyes.

"Well, look at these." His grin was toothy as he took in her vibrant crimson and black underwear. Part lace, part filigree, but entirely sexy, it hugged her so tight, the outline of her folds was clearly visible through the fabric. "Such sexy panties. Did you come out looking to get fucked?" He pushed a finger into the centre of the garment, gently rubbing up and down, tracing the line of her furrow. "Mmm…and you're so wet." His mouth watering at the heady aroma of her arousal, he drew in a long, exaggerated, breath.

"Ja-Jake-oh!"

He licked her through the lace, the point of his tongue sweeping up the cleft in a slow drag up and over her clit, collecting all the creamy dew that had seeped through. It was the briefest tease of contact, but it was enough to make her knees all but buckle as her hips jumped, pleading for more.

"You're so responsive, you dirty girl. Hasn't someone been getting any lately?"

"No-no-no! Please, Jake, don't…"

"Have you fucked anyone else?" Jake repeated, pushing his finger into her heat, then dragging it up to bear down on her clit. "Answer me."

"No! No, there's been no one else! Just- please Jake, I- oh God! Just you. Just you! Don't-don't tease me, I can't-oh fuck, there right there! I can't take it! Eat me! Fuck me! I don't care, just make me cum."

Jake's mouth enveloped the bud of her clit through the lace and he sucked. Hard. He had dreamed of this moment. Of having her beneath him again, at his mercy, begging him to finish her. In those moments he had teased and toyed with her, driven her to the brink of ecstasy, only to pull back and start over. But here, now, he just couldn't deny her.

Instead, he watched the orgasm sweep over her with almost perverse fascination, drinking her in, recommitting every moment to memory. How her skin flushed, the way she arched and thrashed, forcing her eyes shut against the pleasure and worrying her bottom lip to keep from moaning. She was perfect. A deity. The goddess of love, beauty, and debauchery. There was nothing he wouldn't do for her. He was her faithful servant, enslaved to worship at her feet.

Restrained as she was, her release racked her like a storm. Jake sucked her all the way through, her flavour like honeyed wine on his tongue, and as it passed, her legs gave way. Rising up to meet her, he released the hold on her wrists to steady her while his other hand hooked around her thigh, raising one long leg.

"Wrap your leg around me."

She obeyed, but the difference in their heights forced her to raise herself onto the tiptoes of the other leg to do so. Jake dipped his head to take her mouth in a long, lush kiss. Swirling his tongue around hers, the hand that had been holding her leg dipped down to the crotch of his jeans where his cock formed a very obvious bulge. While that hand worked at the buttons, the hand that had been supporting her back teased down the nubs of her spine to cup her bum, two fingers hooking under and drawing back the drenched thong.

When he pulled back, glazed eyes struggled to focus on him "Ja-Jake?"

He swept his tongue across his bottom lip, collecting the last of her heady cream. "Delicious." Then time held its breath.

Holding her gaze, he rolled his hips, watching as Vickey's eyes widened, and that cute little mouth formed a delicious 'O' as his broad crest passed through her folds into lush, welcoming heat.

And it took all his restraint not to lose himself right there.

Jake lived for this moment. When he pushed inside, when their bodies joined, and two came as close to becoming one as it was humanly possible. When he saw the look in her eyes that told him she could feel him inside her. It filled him with a sense of pure primitive conquest. She was his. This beautiful little sex-kitten was all his, and he was going to make sure she knew it. She was his.

"T-too much… s-so big b-bu-but so good!" Vickey panted, her tone pleading and her hands seizing anything she could cling to.

Jake gritted his teeth against his answering moan as her muscles flexed around him, bearing down on his cock. She needed time to adjust, to get used to the feeling of a man inside her again, but he couldn't wait.

He needed her. Now!

She felt as much as heard Jake's low growl of pleasure. The deep rumble hummed through his skin into hers as he pulled back, withdrawing until more than half his length had left her, before driving back home. The sudden delicious shock of deeper penetration had Vickey's head rolling back. "Jake!"

"Yeah, that's it, you missed my cock. Didn't you?" With his hands only half supporting her, he repeated the move.

"Yes!" She couldn't believe this was happening. It was so surreal, like something straight out of a Sylvia Day novel. Jake. Here. Fucking her against the wall in a dark corner of this sleazy Docklands club. And her, utterly helpless to do anything about it, powerless in his arms as he pinned her to the wall. The odd position was making her feel disoriented and her pussy was sucking wantonly on his cock.

God, she had missed this. He was too big for her. Too long. Too thick. It was always a struggle for her to accommodate him, but when he was fully sheathed inside her, he stretched her out and left her feeling completely stuffed. Using what little leverage her one foot could give her to grind herself against him while digging her heel into the base of his spine, she urged him on, craving the raw, primal heat that only Jake could invoke in her.

"Fuck! You feel so good!" he panted. "This has you so hot, knowing anyone could come by and see you getting fucked."

"J-Jake!" She wanted to deny it. But just the vision conjured up by that statement had her ready to burst. Instead, she pushed back and ground her throbbing clit against his pelvis, craving more.

"I'm going to make you scream, love. Make you scream so loud so the whole place will hear you begging me to fuck you, to make you cum." Then he heaved her into the air.

The motion was so quick. So sudden. It made her half squeak in fright and half moan with ecstasy. She was forced to relinquish her hold to throw her arms around his neck, clinging to him with all her might. He had an incredible body, like marble, not bulky, but etched and defined. She longed to see him, to pull those clothes from him and bask in his magnificence and feel his warmth pressing around her. But then he began to pump her up and down, his cock slamming into her with wild abandon.

"Oh fuck! Jake! No! Not so-fuck! I can't-Oh fuck! Yes! Fuck me! Fuck me!" Her voice was rising, growing louder with the sensations stirring in her centre. Desperate to smother the sounds he was drawing out of her, she buried her face in the hollow of his throat to kiss, bite, and suck all the skin she could reach.

God, his strength was amazing. Even pounding into her like a jackhammer, driving into her harder and deeper than before, he supported her so easily as though she weighed less than a feather. Manipulating her. Using her. Controlling her with irresistible force as large hands squeezed her arse hard enough to make her gasp, driving her up and down, his thick cock sawing through her wet heat, touching those places she had never known existed before she'd met this man.

It felt like he would split her in two at any moment.

Anything he wanted, he could have. She was his for the taking. She couldn't take it. It was too good, too much. He was right. She was going to scream. Any moment now, he was going to shove his big dick inside her all the way, bump her clit, and she would shatter and scream for the whole club to hear!

"Jake!" she breathed in his ear, taking her lobe between her teeth, her inner walls squeezing him. "Make me ride your big cock, baby- oh fuck! Oh my God, yes, yes, yes!"

Fuck, this was it. She couldn't stop. He was going to make her cum, and she was going to scream. Oh God, she was going to scream, and she didn't care. Let them all hear. Let them see. She didn't care. She only needed…

"Cum for me, angel." Jake's mouth caught her lips in a searing kiss the instant he thrust up to meet her halfway as he brought her down and buried himself inside her all the way to the root, forcing her over the edge.

The orgasm ripped through her in waves of fire, fast and hard, rippling outward from the pit of her stomach to the tips of her fingers and toes. The scream that left her was voiceless, but she could feel herself shaking. The very fibre of her being was trying to escape the bounds of flesh and soar free to the heavens.

She clung to Jake with everything she had. He was her anchor to the mortal world and seemed content to let her ride the waves of her orgasm until the heat and frenzy ebbed slowly away to leave her floating in the warm comfort she only knew with him. Here, in his arms, she could forget. She could forget about her father and the family he murdered, the old paedophile calling himself *The People's King,* the men hunting her, the bounty.

Whatever he was. However bad he might be for her. Jake made her feel safe and whole. He was the only one who could.

For that, she would love him forever.

Chapter Six

Breathing hard, the black spots still dancing before his eyes from the intensity of his orgasm, Jake held the girl close, savouring the feel of her. It felt so right, her in his arms, holding her. It always did. Even when everything around them was wrong, she felt right.

She was perfect.

"That was… something."

Snuggling closer, Vickey murmured a sleepy "Mmm-" She stiffened, "Oh God."

"Why, thank you, angel, but I'm just a man." The joke came easily to his lips, even as his insides knotted at her tone. Fear? What could she have to be afraid of with him?

"I-I have…" Her voice was weak but the force with which she pushed away from him was as strong as ever. She looked a state. Sweater crumpled and creased. Skin flushed. Hair dishevelled. Lips bruised and swollen. All the hallmarks of a woman who'd just been thoroughly shagged and was about to take the walk of shame. "I have to go."

Jake watched her go about getting dressed, noting with a small sense of satisfaction the way her legs were shaking as she struggled to pull her jeans on while still wearing those slip-on shoes. She didn't look at him. Rather, she seemed to be making a point of looking anywhere but. Then she was gone, stumbling away from him, away from the dark, around a bend into the light as the dance floor beyond was suddenly lit up and shouts and cheers trumpeted *Merry Christmas.*

Jake watched her go. He didn't say a word, only watched with a bemused smile playing across his lips, and when she was gone, he slumped back against the wall. The wall he'd just so readily fucked her against.

He fumbled to do his jeans up with only the slightest care, the task made all the more awkward for the fact he was still hard as a rock. Once was never enough with that girl. He couldn't explain it, but there was just something about her that made him able to go all night. When he was satisfactorily covered, he reached into his pocket and pulled out a box of fags and his old regimental lighter. He shook a cigarette free, took it between his lips and with a practised flick of his wrist and lit the end. Ignoring the *No Smoking* sign hanging barely a metre away, he took a long drag, let out a breath of grey smoke, and began to laugh.

"God, I love you Vickey Romano."

High above, sunken into the ceiling, one of *Seven's* numerous security cameras continued to record.

THIS IS THE END OF **BROKEN**

BUT THIS IS NEITHER THE
BEGINNING, NOR THE END OF
THEIR STORY...

JAKE AND VICKEY WILL RETURN IN

SHATTER

Also by L.M. Mountford

TEMPTATION JUST GOT EVEN SWEETER...
Sweet Temptations:
THE BOSS'S DAUGHTER
THE LORD OF LUST
L.M. MOUNTFORD

*He thought his temptations were over, but they
were only just beginning…*

Until last week, Richard Martin was just another
middle-aged guy. Married to a wife he loved,
father to a son he adored, stuck in a dead-end
job, just counting the days go by…
Then everything changed.
He made a mistake.
Now to save his marriage, he's going to have to
pay the price.
There's just one problem, Scarlet Holmes.
His Supervisor.
She loves to play games with her staff and now,
seeming very aware of his little secret, she wants
to play a game.
And she always gets what she wants.
Because she just so happens to be The Boss's
Daughter.

FORBIDDEN
Desire
CONFESSIONS OF A TROPHY WIFE
BOOK 1
THE LORD OF LUST
L.M. MOUNTFORD

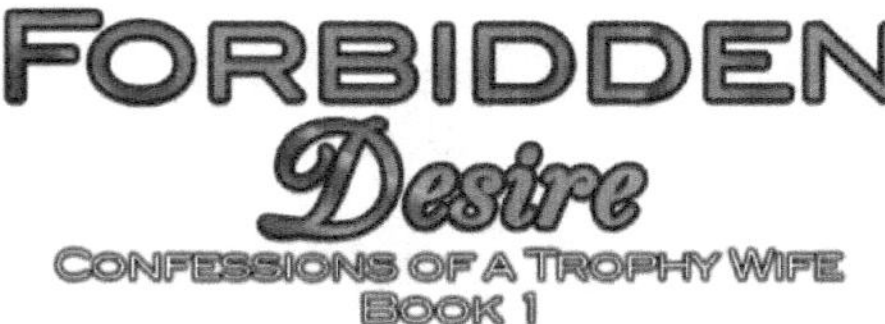

To all the rest of the world, Elizabeth Clarke has it all.
A successful husband. A beautiful home. And now a son off to
university. She is a perfect housewife with the perfect life.
It's a lie.
Her husband is a lying, drinking philanderer who hates her as
much as she loathes him. Her home is beautiful, but empty,
nothing more than a gilded cage to keep her trapped in a world
she never wanted.
That is, until he came back into town.
Hugh Becket.
Her son's best friend. He's hot, young, and so forbidden.
Elizabeth knows she should stay away, but when the devil
comes knocking on her door in the middle of the night, what's a
poor neglected trophy wife to do?

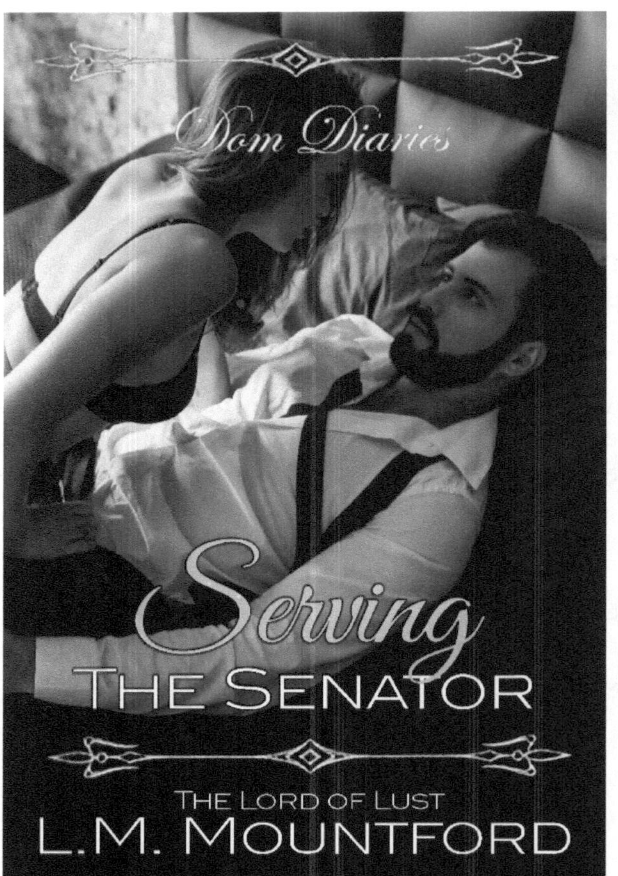

Dom Diaries
Serving
THE SENATOR
THE LORD OF LUST
L.M. MOUNTFORD

He is my Hades
I'd played the role of a goddess, bound and chained for the service of mortals.
He freed me.
He freed me, unchained me and taken me to his underworld, his dark realm where he'd brought out all my forbidden and secret desires.
And now I'm his.
His attendant. His servant…
Serving the Senator is a sizzling new release from the lord of Lust. Loaded with tension and sizzling chemistry, it is a modern reimagining of the ancient myth of Hades and Persephone. A stand-alone romance, it is loaded with scenes of an adult nature that feature BDSM, Dominance play, and so much heat, they may very well melt your e-reader…

DELICIOUSLY SINFUL
Liaisons
A COLLECTION OF HOT AND ORGASMIC STORIES
FROM THE LORD OF LUST
L.M. MOUNTFORD

Deliciously Sinful Liaisons

A collection of hot and orgasmic stories by The Lord of Lust

Do you love hard men, strong women, sizzling chemistry and erotic scenes that make *Fifty Shades of Grey* look like five shades of beige?
Well, here you go...
7 Books, 7 hard and rugged men, 7 sizzling page turners that will have you devouring every word from start to finish...
And for the first time ever, an extract from the lord's long-awaited and much-anticipated sequel to his debut –
Sweet Temptations: The Boss's Daughter

Warning: The stories in this steamy collection are so intense and the scene so hot, they may cause your kindle to melt while reading...

Temptation And Seduction

L.M. MOUNTFORD

Temptation & Seduction

Five tales of Lust, desire & Temptation

L.M. Mountford, The Lord of Lust, brings you a collection of some of his hottest works. 5 of the sexiest stories ever released on Kindle & Ereader...

Plus, for the first time ever, read an extract from the long-awaited sequel to his debut - **Sweet Temptation: The Boss's Daughter**

***** These stories contain descriptions of sexual content, Violence, BDSM, Paranormal, S&M & Dubious Consent for 18+ Adults only*****

REC
THEIR SILENCE COMES AT A PRICE...
UNCOVERED
THE LORD OF LUST
L.M. MOUNTFORD

UNCOVERED
L. M. MOUNTFORD

My stepbrother and I have always been close, sometimes we were VERY close.

*It was our little secret, until his friends walked in on us. Now they know our secret and **they want to play too...***

When Mina returns for her stepbrother's 21st birthday, she thinks her days of lusting after him are over. Caught up in the heat and passion of the moment, she is stunned to find them back in bed together; their feelings clearly far from resolved. Haunted by her desire, Mina now has another problem… she must head down a path of lust and desire; torn between the dark delights of the handsome bad boy down the street and her adorable stepbrother who has always been there for her. Can she confront the truth she has long tried to bury? How far will she go to save the one she wants, but knows she can never truly have?

A full length, 40,000+ word novel, Uncovered is the stand-alone erotic drama from the Author of the sinfully delicious, Sweet Temptations Trilogy. Warning! It contains adult themes, harsh language, and graphic content, descriptions of intense sexual scenes, and dubcon (dubious consent) that might be triggers for some readers.

Sweet
Temptations:
THE BABYSITTER
Temptation has never been so sweet...
L.M. MOUNTFORD

SWEET TEMPTATIONS

Meet Richard Martin. Tall, dark and handsome; he's well mannered, married to his beautiful university sweetheart, works in a job he can't stand with people who infuriate him, and so sexually frustrated he's about ready to blow like Mount Vesuvius...

Enter Rebecca, Scarlet and Samantha, three sirens sent by God to plague and tempt him. Will he be able to do what's right and resist their advances, or will these temptresses lure him to the rocks?

In this first volume in Dark Inferno's sizzling new series: Sweet Temptations, A naughty babysitter sets out to seduce her man. No matter what his wife might think, sweet and innocent, but also seductive and sexy, this tempting siren will rock your world while babysitting your kids and she is determined to lure her man into her bed...

Together In
SYDNEY

LM Mountford

Together In SYDNEY

LM Mountford

I may have been a bad influence on her when we were kids, but this new side of her is going to ruin me...

They were the best of friends. Then they shared a night of passion and in the morning she was gone and Alex has spent years trying to move on.

But then an email arrives out of the blue and suddenly he finds himself boarding the first plane bound for Australia with nothing but his passport and an overnight bag. He's no idea what he'll do, or he's going to say, but one thing's for sure...

He's not going home without her.

Together in Sydney is a Second Chance Romance full of steamy scenes and bad language. It's only recommended for readers 18+. No cliffhanger. Guaranteed HEA!

An erotic PNR/Vampire story by
LM Mountford
Blood
Lust
The Thirst always
wins...

BLOOD LUST

Sooner or later, the thirst always wins...
After a thousand years, Lucian had given up any interest in the
world. His only concern that night was finding his next drink,
preferably from a flavoursome twenty-something with loose
morals and no expectations. Then he saw her...
Kate is just a girl from the country, who came to the city with her
brother to find a life away from their parents' car crash. That is
until the police came knocking on her door one morning and
ripped her new life apart.
Now she has nothing and no one, with only one on her mind...
When these worlds collide, and the things that go bump in the
night come calling, can these two mend the rifts in each other
and give them what they need?

Blood Lust *is a sizzling-hot Paranormal romance. If you like strong-*
willed, sassy heroines and oh-so-bad, drop-dead gorgeous Vampire
heroes with lots of bite, you'll love this page turner.

TRAINING
Tracey

THE LORD OF LUST
L.M. MOUNTFORD

TRAINING TRACEY

I know it's wrong to want my best friend's dad... but what about when his wife offers to share?

Tracey has known the Burtons practically all her life.

They're her best friend's parents.

When she was a little girl they took her on days out to the beach. But she's a woman now, and they have some very important lessons to teach her...

*** Training Tracey is A wicked and uber-hot coming-of-age menage, filled with MF, FF & MFF scenes from the Lord of Lust's Dark and Dirty alter ego. There is NO cheating, NO cliffhanger and a guaranteed HEA with plenty of steam.***

WARNING 18+: This book is erotic and contains material that may be considered offensive to some readers, which includes graphic language, explicit sex, and adult situations.

Just Once
A FRIENDS TO LOVERS ROMANCE
L.M. MOUNTFORD

Just Once

They were the very poster children for the boy and girl next door, if a couple of streets apart.

Friends for longer than forever. They'd walked to school together. He'd protected her from the bullies when they teased her about her glasses. She'd tended to his cuts and bruises when he fell. He pushed her to try new things. She snuck looks at him when he wasn't looking.

All her life, Faye had loved Terry, but he was oblivious. He's her best friend, her closest friend, but he's oblivious and now he has a Girlfriend. All day long, she has to watch them together and it's killing her. She wants him, all of him, but he's taken. So, instead, she wants one night. Just once, one night, between friends.

One night, just once...

Play Time
Books 1&2
DARK INFERNO

Play Time Books 1 & 2

Play Time: Double Period combines Naughty Students, Magic Girls & Demonic Succubus Teachers that will suck you dry and leave you begging for another round.

Here both the titillating Paranormal Erotica Hit and it's sequel, Extra Credit are available like never before in a 30,000+ word lesson in submission, BDSM and Fem Domination that will have you hooked page after page.

Valentine
Misadventures
LM Mountford

VALENTINE MISADVENTURES

There is one name that can inspire fear all along the East Coast.

A lord of the Underworld. A Napoleon of crime... Mr Larry.

And his daughter is on the run from him.

Sophie has lived all her life in her father's shadow. She's an underworld princess. Her future has already been set up and laid before her and she knows there can be no escape.

Then she met Luke.

He's everything she ever wanted in a man. Tough, strong, and absolutely devoted to her. There's just one problem. He's her bodyguard, and there's no place for an affair with a scrapper from the hard streets in her future.

So when they're caught, they have no choice but to flee. Now they're on the run, hunted by all sides. Can their love survive? Can they survive?